The text in this edition of *Polar Bear, Polar Bear, What Do You Hear?* has been reformatted for beginning readers.

---

The Eric Carle Museum of Picture Book Art was built to celebrate the art that we are first exposed to as children. Located in Amherst, Massachusetts, the 40,000-square-foot museum is the first in the United States devoted to national and international picture book art.

Visit www.carlemuseum.org

---

Visit mackids.com/series/MyFirstReader/BillMartinJr
to learn about Bill Martin Jr's approach to reading.

Henry Holt and Company
*Publishers since 1866*
120 Broadway,
New York, NY 10271
mackids.com



Library of Congress Cataloging-in-Publication Data
Martin, Bill, 1916–2004.
Polar bear, polar bear, what do you hear? / by Bill Martin, Jr.;
pictures by Eric Carle.—1st My first reader ed.
p. cm.
"My first reader."
Summary: Zoo animals from polar bear to walrus make their distinctive
sounds for each other, while children imitate the sounds for the zookeeper.
Includes note to parents and teachers, and related activities.
ISBN 978-0-8050-9245-5 (paper over board : alk. paper)
[1. Stories in rhyme. 2. Animal sounds—Fiction. 3. Zoo animals—Fiction.]
I. Carle, Eric, ill. II. Title.
PZ8.3.M418Pm 2010 [E]—dc22 2009044269

First hardcover edition—1991
First My First Reader edition—2010
Printed in China by RR Donnelley Asia Printing Solutions Ltd., Dongguan City, Guangdong Province.

10 9 8 7

My First Reader 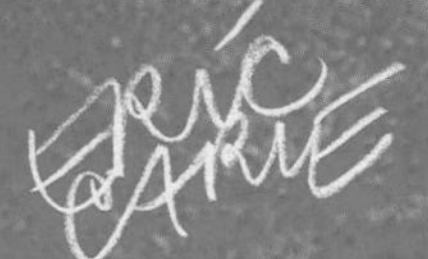

# POLAR BEAR, POLAR BEAR, WHAT DO YOU HEAR?

By Bill Martin Jr
Pictures by Eric Carle

Henry Holt and Company · New York

Polar Bear,
Polar Bear,
what do you hear?

I hear a lion
roaring in my ear.

Lion,
Lion,
what do you hear?

I hear a hippopotamus
snorting in my ear.

Hippopotamus,
Hippopotamus,
what do you hear?

I hear a flamingo
fluting in my ear.

Flamingo,
Flamingo,
what do you hear?

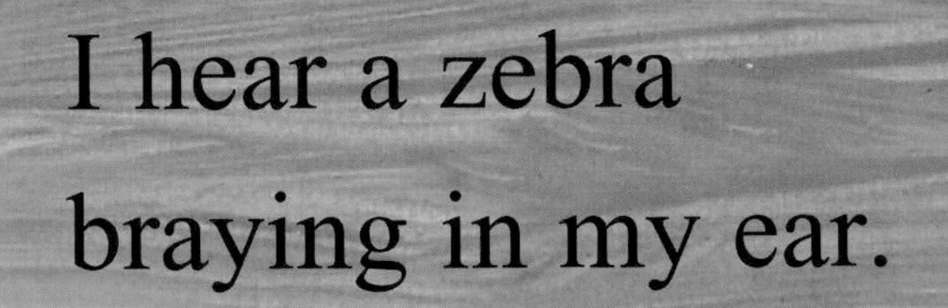

I hear a zebra
braying in my ear.

Zebra,
Zebra,
what do you hear?

I hear a boa constrictor
hissing in my ear.

Boa Constrictor,
Boa Constrictor,
what do you hear?

I hear an elephant
trumpeting in my ear.

Elephant,
Elephant,
what do you hear?

I hear a leopard
snarling in my ear.

Leopard,
Leopard,
what do you hear?

I hear a peacock
yelping in my ear.

Peacock,
Peacock,
what do you hear?

I hear a walrus
bellowing in my ear.

Walrus,
Walrus,
what do you hear?

I hear a zookeeper
whistling in my ear.

Zookeeper,
Zookeeper,
what do you hear?

I hear children . . .

growling like a polar bear,
roaring like a lion,
snorting like a hippopotamus,
fluting like a flamingo,
braying like a zebra,
hissing like a boa constrictor,
trumpeting like an elephant,
snarling like a leopard,
yelping like a peacock,
bellowing like a walrus . . .

that's what I hear.

Dear Parents and Teachers,

*Polar Bear, Polar Bear, What Do You Hear?* is a patterned, question-and-answer book. These qualities can be helpful to children learning to read because the repetitive language along with word clues in Eric Carle's pictures help children to predict what happens next, to remember the story, and to learn to read many of the words easily.

Here are some ways that you might use this book with children:

- ✦ Before opening the book, talk about the polar bear on the cover. Ask, "What might Polar Bear hear?"
- ✦ Next, turn the pages and enjoy the bold collage art together. Ask, "What do you know about this animal?"
- ✦ After you read and reread the story many times, pause before an animal or a sound word and encourage your child to supply that word. If your child doesn't chime in, try again on another day.
- ✦ See the following pages for more activities.

When your child says, "I want to read this book by myself!" celebrate the reading and listen with enthusiasm as your child reads it again and again.

—Laura Robb
*Educator and Reading Consultant*

What animal names
can you read?

polar bear

lion

hippopotamus

flamingo

zebra

Can you match the words to the pictures?

boa constrictor

elephant

leopard

peacock

walrus

What sound words can you read?

growl

roar

snort

flute

bray

Can you make
these sounds?

hiss

trumpet

snarl

yelp

bellow

Which animals like
to be in cold places?

Which animals like
to be in warm places?

Which animals
like both?

Which animals like
to be in water?

Which animals like
to stay on land?

Which animals
like both?

ERIC CARLE